The Hungry
Snowman

CHEX BOOKS NEW YORK

It had been snowing hard all
night. By morning the snow lay
white and deep over everything.
Sam looked out of his bedroom
window. He felt very excited.
He ran downstairs to find
his mother.
"May I go and play outside?"
he asked. "It looks great fun!"
"All right," said his mother.
"But put on your gloves and
scarf. It's very cold."

Sam ran outside and met
his friends. Soon they were
playing in the snow. They began
to throw snowballs at each other.
Then Sam said, "Let's build
a snowman!"
"Here's some coal for his eyes,"
said Jim.
"And a carrot for his nose,"
said Jenny.
"He looks almost real," said Sam.
He put his scarf around the
snowman's neck.

"Dinnertime!" called Sam's
mother. Sam went back indoors.
Outside all was very quiet.
Very, very slowly the snowman began
to move. He looked around carefully
to make sure no one was about.
Then he said crossly, "It's all right
for Sam, but no one worries
about my dinner. They must know
that a snowman gets hungry too!".

A squirrel ran into the garden.
She was carrying some nuts.
"Hello," said the snowman.
"May I share your dinner?
I'm very hungry."
The squirrel dropped her nuts
in surprise. A talking snowman!
"You can have some nuts if you
like," she said. "They are
very nice."
"Oh dear!" said the snowman.
"They're much too hard. I cannot
eat these for my dinner."

A rabbit hopped into the garden.
"Hello," said the snowman.
"What do you eat?"
The rabbit looked at the snowman's
nose and laughed.
"I like carrots best of all!" he said.
"Oh dear!" cried the snowman.
"That's no good. I can't eat
my own nose!"
"Don't worry," said the rabbit.
"There are plenty of other things
to eat."

The snowman looked up. He saw
a robin sitting on the branch
of a tree. It was singing merrily.
"Hello," said the snowman.
"You sound happy today."
"It's because this tree is full
of juicy berries for me to eat,"
said the robin. "Why don't
you try some?"
"Oh no, I can't," said the snowman.
"Only birds can eat those.
Oh, I am so hungry. What shall I do?"

Then a wonderful smell began to
fill the air. It was coming from
the kitchen. The snowman walked
slowly across the garden.
He looked into the kitchen.
He could see Sam's mother baking
cookies and icing cakes. The sight
of them made the snowman's
mouth water.
"That's what I would like to eat!"
he cried. "I'll just have to wait
until nobody is looking!"

Later that night, when everyone was asleep, the snowman tiptoed into the kitchen. He opened the refrigerator door and found a large plate of cream cakes. "These taste wonderful!" he said, happily helping himself. "Much better than nuts and berries!" He ate some cookies. Then he ate a bowl of ice cream. Feeling much better, he crept back outside without a sound.

The next morning Sam's mother
was very surprised. All of her
cream cakes were missing.
"And someone has taken all the
cookies, too!" she said.
"Was it you, Sam?"
"Not me," said Sam.
"And look at these big wet
footprints on the floor,"
she said crossly. "Where have
they come from?"

Every night the snowman crept
into the house for his dinner.
Every morning Sam's mother
asked where her food had gone.
"First it was cream cakes and
ice cream," she said. "But now
all the cold ham and turkey
has disappeared, too!"
Sam looked at the wet footprints.
They led outside. Sam looked
at the snowman. "I'm sure he's
getting fatter," he said.

One night the snowman ate far
too much.
"I'll sit here and rest," he said.
Soon he was fast asleep. Hours
later he woke up. He was lying
in a pool of water.
"Oh no!" he cried. "I'm melting!"
He was too weak to reach
the door.
"I'll hide in the refrigerator,"
he said. "It's cold in there!"
As he climbed in, the door
slammed shut!

The next morning Sam ran out into the garden. He couldn't believe his eyes. His snowman had disappeared! His mother was in the kitchen mopping up a pool of water.

"Something very odd is going on here," she said. "I'll check the refrigerator." She opened the door and gasped in amazement. Inside was the snowman, only he was much, much smaller!

"How did he get in there?"
asked Sam. "Look how small he is!"
He carried the snowman outside.
"You'd better stay here from now on,"
he said, smiling. "I'll bring
out some food for you. So don't
try any more tricks."
The snowman had learned his lesson.
After his narrow escape
he decided he was much safer
outside where he belonged.
He decided never to steal food
from the kitchen again!

Say these words again

snow	nuts
deep	branch
coal	berries
carrot	cakes
scarf	wet
dinner	fatter
squirrel	smaller